Professor Hinkle performs a magic show for schoolchildren one cold winter day.

What's in Professor Hinkle's magic hat?

Professor Hinkle is not a good magician.

Hocus Pocus, the rabbit, pops out of Professor Hinkle's hat.

Paint what you think the children are making in the snow.

The children make a snowman!

Paint your own magic hat on the snowman.

Hocus Pocus gives Karen the magic hat.

The magic hat makes Frosty come to life!

When Frosty wakes up, he cheers,
"Happy birthday!"

Decorate your own snowman!

Paint what you think
Professor Hinkle is thinking.

Professor Hinkle wants his magic hat back!

Professor Hinkle grabs the magic hat from Frosty's head!

Karen tells Professor Hinkle to give
the magic hat back.

Professor Hinkle's hat hops away!

Paint something silly on Professor Hinkle's head.

Hocus Pocus runs off with the magic hat!

HOCUS

POCUS

Frosty comes back to life!

Frosty merrily juggles snowballs.

Paint colorful Christmas presents for Frosty to juggle.

Frosty and the children dance!

Frosty leads a parade through town.

Paint yourself in the parade with Frosty.

Paint a sun rising high in the sky.

It's getting hot! Fill the thermometer with red.

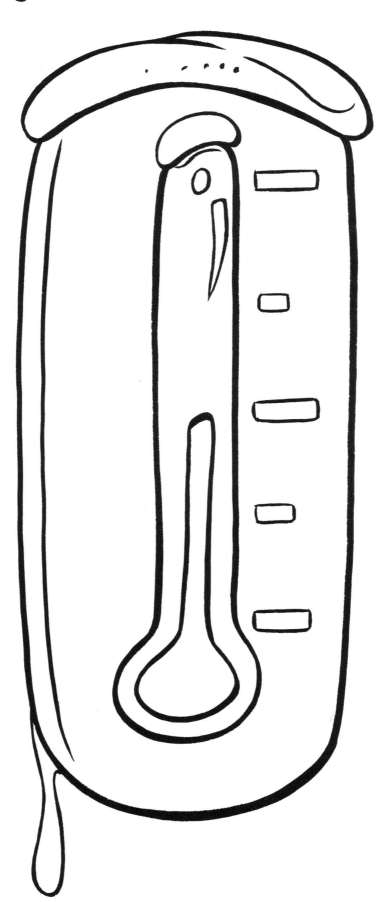

WINTER IS WONDERFUL!

Frosty is worried that he might melt.

Karen knows how to keep Frosty from melting!

Frosty can ride the train to where it is colder.

**Frosty and Karen don't
have any money for a ticket.**

Woo-woo! The train is ready to leave the station.

Frosty and Karen ride in the train's freezer car.

Karen is c-c-c-cold!

Run! Professor Hinkle is on the train, too!

Frosty is worried that Karen is sick.

Hocus Pocus knows who can help—Santa!

Karen needs a fire to keep warm. Add wood and flames to the scene.

Paint the correct path for Frosty and Karen to escape from Professor Hinkle.

Frosty takes Karen into a hothouse to warm up.

Karen feels better, thanks to Frosty!

Paint your own colorful hothouse flower.

Professor Hinkle locks Frosty in the hothouse!

Karen tells Frosty
that everything will be all right.

It's too hot. Frosty melts!

Professor Hinkle takes his hat back.

Santa arrives just in time!

Professor Hinkle gives the magic hat back.

With the magic hat and a little cold
winter wind, Frosty returns!

Santa and Karen are delighted to see Frosty again.

Frosty and his friends dance!

CHRISTMAS HUGS!

Karen will see Frosty again next Christmas!

Paint some decorations for the Christmas tree.

Merry Christmas!